Happy Hooves
Yuk!

For Lachie and Ella.
A.B.

For Sophie, Oli and Tom. xxx
R.E.

First published in 2016 by Fat Fox Books ltd

fatfoxbooks.com

ISBN: 978-1910884065

Fat Fox and associated logos are trademarks and/or registered trademarks of Fat Fox Books Ltd.

Printed and bound in Slovenia.

Happy Hooves
Yuk!

A. Bogie   Rebecca Elliott

fatfoxbooks.com

The sun was shining high in the sky,
As happy Pig relaxed with a **sigh.**

He was having a lovely time,
Rolling in gloopy mud and grime.

But all of a sudden his tummy grumbled,
Like a thunder crash, it loudly **rumbled.**
The growl came deep inside his belly,
Making it wobble like strawberry jelly.

'Well,' said Pig, 'I must make some tea,
All I've eaten today is a flea.
My favourite friends must be starving too,
That grass they munch, can't be nice to chew.'

An idea began to form in Pig's head:
He would make his friends a delicious spread.
Some yummy food for everyone,
A farmyard party, oh what fun!

With happy hooves, he blew up balloons,
Planned silly games and chose some tunes.
He went to collect some tasty bugs,
A caterpillar, worm and a few fat slugs.

When all the food was ready to eat,
Pig told his friends about the treat.
They gathered together, quick as a flash,
Ready to start his scrumptious bash.

'Now, Cow,' said Pig, 'try this tasty meal,
You'll like it so much I think you'll squeal!

I've used my Grandma's secret recipe,
To make this fabulous worm spaghetti!'

'Yuk!' said Cow, 'I can't eat a worm!
I just couldn't bear to feel it squirm.
To wriggle about, slither and slide,
I don't want a worm wiggling inside!'

'Please,' said Cow, 'don't be offended,
I'd rather eat grass, it's really quite splendid.'
Pig was confused, 'But worms make you strong,
And they help my snout grow hairy and long.'

'Well Foal, I think you'll find this yummy,
In fact, you'll say it's super scrummy.
This recipe here, you mustn't hurry,
In front of you is my hot snail curry.'

'Yuk!' said Foal. 'I can't eat a snail,
It sounds disgusting and will make me wail.
It would be crunchy and rather smelly,
And all that slime would be in my belly.'

'I'm sorry,' said Foal, 'don't be upset,
I'd rather eat hay, so please don't fret.'
Pig was puzzled, 'You won't try my snails?
But that's how pigs get their curly tails.'

'Still, Donkey, I know you'll like my next platter
Because – just for you – it's smothered in batter!
The main ingredient pinches and nips,
But don't be alarmed – these are earwig chips!'

'YUK!' said Donkey, 'I can't eat an earwig,
It would pinch and really hurt me, Pig.
Earwigs have nasty pincers that tweak,
It would squeeze and squeeze,
                    making me shriek.'

'I'm sorry,' said Donkey, 'don't be sad,
I'd rather eat weeds, they're not too bad!'
Pig was baffled, 'Aren't you aware?
Earwigs can toughen your

teeth, I swear!'

'Fine then, Sheep, you'll love this dinner,
The recipe here is quite a winner.
It's also very good for you,
Please try my delicious green **frog** stew.'

'Yuk!' said Sheep, 'I can't eat a frog,
It was croaking earlier upon that log!
It would hop about, jump and leap,
I'd never be able to go to sleep!'

'Don't mind me, there is clover to chew,
I'd rather eat that, then there's more for you.'
Pig was perplexed, 'Yes, frogs jump

But they keep my tum so round and plump.'

Now he felt sad and started to blub,
'Oh Pig,' they cried,
    'we like different grub.

There'll be some food we all enjoy,
Let's have a think, don't worry old boy.'

'I've got it!' said Pig, 'Maybe this dish
Will make us all shout out: DELISH!

This final bowl fixes bellyache,
Everyone try my chocolate mud cake!'

'Yumbellina!'

they yelled, 'That's perfect Pig!
It's so delicious we want to jig.
Now turn up the music, let's start to bop,
We hope this party will never stop!'